What's this page for?

It's called the endpaper, but it always comes at the beginning.

This book is dedicated to my
friend, Dr. Dan (Medicine Man)
who provided me with the
opportunity to do less. (CF)

First published in Great Britain in 2014 by
words & pictures, an imprint of Quarto Publishing Plc,
6 Blundell Street, London N7 9BH

First paperback published in Great Britain in 2015

978-1-91027-713-3

A CIP catalogue record for this book is available from the British Library

1 3 5 7 9 8 6 4 2

Printed in China

THE CAT, THE DOG, LITTLE RED, THE EXPLODING EGGS, THE WOLF AND GRANDMA'S WARDROBE

Diane and Christyan Fox

words & pictures

Little Red Riding Hood

There was once a sweet little maid who lived with her father and mother in a pretty little cottage at the edge of the village.

She always wore a red cloak with a hood, which suited her so well that everybody called her Little Red Riding Hood.

What's this?

It's a story about a little girl who always wears a red cloak with a hood.

COOL! I love stories
about superheroes.
What's her
special power?

She doesn't have
any special powers.
It's not that kind
of a story.

And can you stop
doing that, please?

So, what
happens?

Well, one morning
her mother asked
Red Riding Hood to
take a basket of
eggs, butter, cake,
and dainties to
her grandmother.

So, kindness is
her special power?
Does she hypnotize
bad guys into
being nice?

And what's
a "dainty"?

A dainty is like a...
well... it's a kind
of small... er...

Look, do you
want to hear this
story or not?

So, where was I?

Little Red Riding Hood was on her way to Grandma's house when she met a wolf...

A WOLF! EXCELLENT!

They're always the bad guys in stories like this.

I bet she zaps him with her **KINDNESS RAY**.

ZZZZ!!

She does **NOT** have a
KINDNESS RAY...
she has a basket of
eggs and butter and
cakes and dainties.

How does she fight
crime, then? Is it
like a cool kind of
flying gadget basket?
  Are they exploding
eggs? Can she whack
him with a dainty?

THERE'S **<u>NO</u>** KINDNESS RAY,
<u>NO</u> FLYING BASKET
AND **<u>NO</u>** EXPLODING EGGS.

SHE'S JUST A SWEET
LITTLE GIRL WITH
TERRIBLE FASHION SENSE
ON HER WAY TO SEE
HER GRANDMOTHER.

OK, OK...
so let's hear
the rest of
the story.

Well, the Wolf asked
Red Riding Hood where
she was going and she
said, "Grandma's house,"
so the Wolf said goodbye
and secretly headed off
to Grandma's house...

Hang on...

why doesn't the
Wolfman try to
eat Hood Girl
there and then?

You're doing this
on purpose,
aren't you?
How should I
know why he
didn't try to
eat her?

Hmm...
I wonder if
it's because
old ladies taste
better than
little girls?

Anyway, the Wolf arrived at Grandma's cottage and saw the old lady lying in bed. She jumped up when she saw the Wolf and locked herself in the wardrobe.

I think the Wolf needs to think bigger if he's going to be a super-villain.

Maybe he could rob a bank on the way to Grandma's house?

Yep.

OK, so Grandma leapt up out of bed and locked herself in the wardrobe to be safe.

Then the Wolf put on some of Grandma's clothes and climbed into the bed, waiting for Little Red Riding Hood to arrive.

Hang on...

so now you're saying he DOES want to eat her?

Yes... anyway, this is my favourite bit. She arrived and said, "What big eyes you have Grandma," and the Wolf replied, "All the better to see you with."

She's not very bright, is she? I mean, if there were a Wolf dressed up as MY grandma, I might have noticed right away.

...and Little Red Riding Hood said, "What a big nose you have, Grandma."

And the Wolf replied, "All the better to smell you with, my dear."

Let me see that book...

...And she said, "What big teeth you have, Grandma," and the Wolf said...

ALL THE BETTER TO EAT YOU UP!

YIKES!

But just at the last moment,
Little Red Riding Hood's
father arrived and

CHOPPED OFF THE WOLF'S HEAD WITH AN AXE!

GULP!

And they all
lived happily
ever after.

I'm not sure
that the Wolf
was very happy
in the end.

So, let's see if I have this right...

The Red Hood is on her way to help an old lady when she meets the Wolfman, whose evil plan it is to eat all the old ladies in the world because he likes dressing up in girls' clothes. He and Red have a big battle over the dainties and Red's father chops Wolfie with an axe.

Well... sort of...

It's not a very
nice story, is it?

Are you absolutely
sure this is a
children's book?

RIGHT, THAT'S IT...
I'm leaving.
Find your own
books to read.

Just one
last
question...

What?

Is Grandma
still in the
wardrobe?
.
.
.

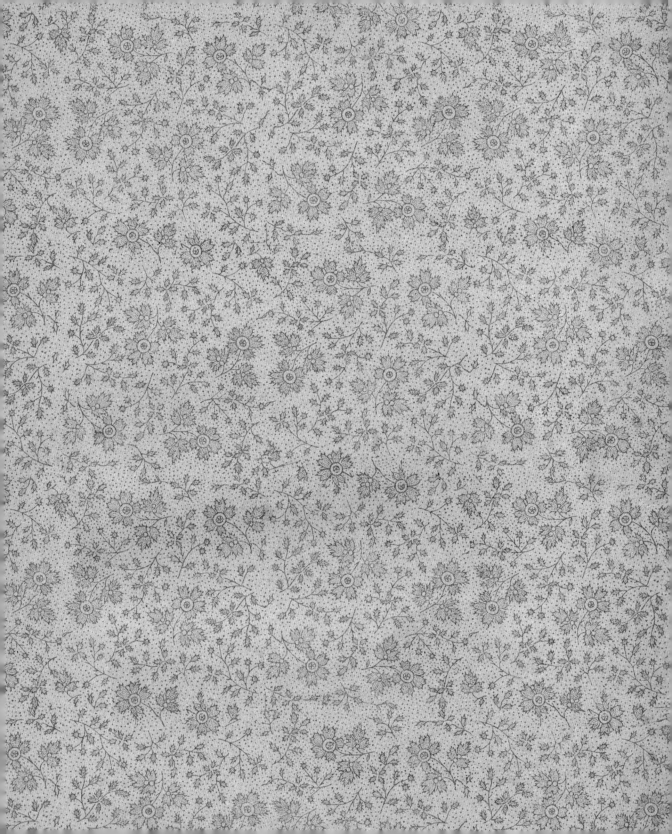

So, do these endpaper things always come at the beginning?

Yes. Unless they're at the end.